Text and illustrations by Michal Hudak. Text of song by Annika Hudak.

The Scripture selections are taken from the New American Bible © 1991, 1986, 1970 by the Confraternity of Christian Doctrine, 3211 Fourth Street, N.E., Washington, DC 20017-1194, U.S.A., and are used by license of the copyright owner. All rights reserved.

This book is published in Swedish by Verbum Förlag, Stockholm, Sweden, under the title *Kalabaliken i Bethlehem* © 2001 by Michal Hudak and Verbum Förlag. All rights reserved.

1   2   3   4   5   6   7   8

ISBN 0-8146-2774-9

MICHAL HUDAK

The Uproar in Bethlehem

A Liturgical Press Book

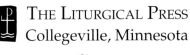 THE LITURGICAL PRESS
Collegeville, Minnesota

www.litpress.org

"Wow! There are a lot of people walking on the roads! Where is everybody going?
What is happening?" wonders Little Figge with the black ears, as do the other sheep.
They are grazing in the meadow outside Bethlehem. The shepherd also wonders:
"So many people are coming and going. It probably has something to do with the Emperor's
command to register. I should go and register, and also register my sheep."

On the way to Bethlehem, the shepherd meets his friends, the goatherd and the cowherd. "Have you seen all the people that are coming and going?" he asks them. "The Emperor in Rome wants everybody to register in the town from which their ancestors came. Come, let us go to Bethlehem and register!"

Bethlehem is crowded. The registrar's table stands in the middle of the marketplace. The merchants have set up their stands. All those who have come need food and perhaps new bottles or baskets. The houses are so crammed full of people that their corners are creaking.

"The likes of you shall not come here among the people! Certainly not with your animals! Are you trying to make fun of His Majesty, the Emperor Gaius Julius Octavius Augustus, in Rome?" the registrar shouts. "Clear off, or else I will call the soldiers!"

The herders, the sheep, the goats, and the cow and the calf
are afraid and run for their lives. Catastrophe! They run into the stands
and are entangled in the ropes. They stumble over bottles and baskets.
Grapes, figs, spices, and melons fly in all directions. They overturn the
registrar's table. Little Figge has fallen into a sack of flour, and his
black ears are now white. He sneezes and sneezes.
Finally, they find the way out of Bethlehem!

Far outside the walls of Bethlehem they stop.
"Oh, oh, oh! The Emperor won't have anything to do with us!
What are we to do now? Let's look for a place where we can stay for the night.
It might be cold tonight," the little goatherd says and makes a fire.
The sheep, the goats, and the cow and the calf are still upset,
and they brush themselves free of flour, figs, spices, melon,
and everything else that they have brought from the marketplace.
Little Figge has stopped sneezing. Soon everything becomes
quiet and peaceful around the fire.
The stars light up one after the other,
and the air is full of pleasant scents
and the chirping of
grasshoppers.

In the middle of the night, they wake up!
It is light, and the air is glittering and blazing in
every shade of color. "What is happening?" wonders
Little Figge and his friends. "Is the registrar coming?"
The herders too become afraid and look for their sticks
and staffs. Then suddenly a shining angel stands in front of them and says: "Do not
be afraid; for behold, I proclaim to you good news of great joy that will be for all the
people. For today in the city of David a savior has been born for you who is
Messiah and Lord. And this will be a sign for you; you will
find an infant wrapped in swaddling clothes and
lying in a manger."

Many angels come down from heaven and start to sing and dance
for the herders, the sheep, the goats, and the cow and the calf.
"Glory to God in the highest and on earth peace
on those on whom his favor rests," they sing.

The herders and all the animals are confused by everything they see and hear. The little
cowherd whispers quietly in the shepherd's ear: "What's a 'flavior'? And who's the 'Messiah'?"
"No not 'flavior,' but 'Savior,'" the shepherd answers quietly. "The scholars tell us that it says
in the old books that one day a new king will come who will be called the Messiah.
He will deliver us, that means save us," he continues thoughtfully.

When the angels have left, the herders say in chorus:
"David's town—that's Bethlehem! Let's go to the town again and look for the baby who is the
Messiah and tell everybody what we have seen and heard." They leave in the middle of the night
with all their sheep, goats, and the cow and the calf. Little Figge stumbles along in the darkness
and wonders: "What does a Messiah look like? The manger must be made of gold and
precious stones. How exciting everything is—angels singing, bright lights,
and a little baby who will save us!"

In Bethlehem the herders knock at doors and windows and ask: "Has the Messiah been born here tonight? We have met some angels, and they told us about him. May we see the little king?"

Little Figge and his friends turn bottles and stands, boxes and sacks, upside down, just to be the first to find the baby in the the golden manger.

Now the
awakened people of
the town get angry and
scream and throw things at the
shepherd, Little Figge, and his friends.
All these stupid herders and their nasty-smelling
animals! "Have you gone mad? What's the matter
with you? Angels, ha! No baby has been here, no
Messiah either. Clear off! We want to sleep!"

Now they are running away from Bethlehem.
They stop far outside the walls of the town. They are breathless and don't know what to do.
Then they suddenly discover a little gleam of light in the darkness. They start walking toward
the light, and they get closer and closer. "It's coming from our old tumbledown stable that we don't use
anymore," the cowherd says. "What's that noise we hear coming from the stable?"

It is a baby crying.
The baby is lying in a manger and is wrapped in swaddling
clothes, just as the angel told them. The baby's parents look in surprise at the herders
and the animals. The shepherd asks: "Who are you?" "I'm Joseph, and this is Mary," the man
answers. "We're from Nazareth and have come to Bethlehem to register. Then Mary felt that it was
time to give birth to the child. Since there wasn't any room for us in Bethlehem, we had to walk on.
It was good that we found this stable. Do we have to leave now?" The shepherd puts Joseph's
and Mary's minds at rest and tells them that they can stay as long as they want.
The shepherd tells them what they have experienced in the meadow.

"But nobody wants to believe us!" they sigh. Mary shows them the baby, who will be called "Jesus." Little Figge is standing near the manger and is thinking, "Is this a Messiah? Can such a baby, born in a stable, be a king? The manger isn't made of gold and precious stones either, and where is the gold crown? Here there is only an ordinary manger made of wood on an earthen floor and heaps of cow dung."

"We haven't any gifts with us for the newborn king," the shepherd says anxiously, and scratches his head with his staff. "But we can give of what we have," he says. Then he takes bread out of his pocket. The goatherd takes out a big piece of cheese, and the cowherd rummages in his big bag for some figs. When they have offered the gifts, they take out their flutes and start playing and singing.

They play so beautifully that Jesus stops crying and falls asleep. The song they are playing and singing is the one that they learned from the angels who came to them in the meadow.

Little Figge's legs begin to twitch. He and his friends start singing and dancing.

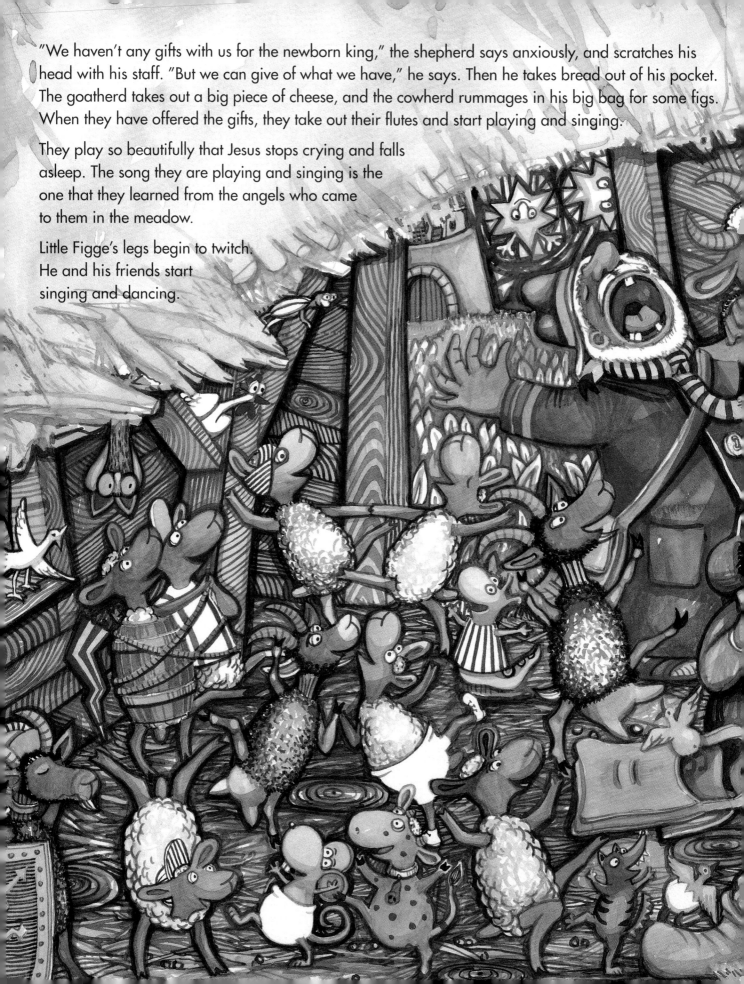

What fun it is to sing and dance for the newborn king!
"Now we must go in to Bethlehem and tell the others about all this,"
the shepherd says. Happily they go to Bethlehem for the third time
where they stand in the middle of the marketplace and sing, call out, bleat, moo,
and dance out their message: "Hurrah! Hurrah! Listen, everybody!
We have found the newborn Messiah, the Savior!"

Gloria

Angels sing:

Text and music: Annika Hudak

Glo-ri, glo-ri, glo-ri, glo-ri, glo-ri - a! Glo-ri - a — —

— ! Glo-ri, glo-ri, glo-ri, glo-ri, glo-ri - a! Glo-ri - a

— — — — ! Glo-ri - a —

— — — — !

Herders and animals sing:

O what is this? Has heav-en been o-pened here?

O what a song! We must go at once to-night! We want to

see the king who is some - where near-by. May-be now